This Little Tiger book
belongs to:

_____

_____

_____

For Elliott – S S

For David and his
MONSTER motorbike – J D

LITTLE TIGER PRESS
1 The Coda Centre, 189 Munster Road, London SW6 6AW

First published in Great Britain 2011
This edition published 2012

ISBN 978-1-84895-228-7
LTP/1800/0395/0312
Printed in China
2 4 6 8 10 9 7 5 3 1

MY MONSTER DUMPER TRUCK

Steve Smallman   Joëlle Dreidemy

LITTLE TIGER PRESS
London

And trundle through the country with the back all full of muck.

RUMBLE...
RUMBLE...

When I am a
grown-up I will drive
a DUMPER TRUCK...

And trundle through the country with the back all full of muck.

RUMBLE...

PUMBLE...

Well, I shall drive a tractor that is BIG and STRONG and FAST...

Well, then I'll be the driver of a massive, MONSTER CRANE. I'll lift your tractor really high, then drop it down AGAIN.

Well, then I'll be the driver of a massive, MONSTER CRANE. I'll lift your tractor really high, then drop it down AGAIN.

CRASH!

CLATTER!

CLATTER!

CLA

Then I will drive a steamroller.
What do you think of THAT?
I'll push your crane right over
and then squash it till it's FLAT!

Hmmmm

mmmmmmmm . . .

Well, actually, I think I'll ride
a motorbike INSTEAD
And vroom along the road with
a big helmet on my HEAD.

But then I'll drive a sports car
that's as fast as FAST CAN BE,
And your silly little motorbike
won't keep up with ME!

Then I will fly a spaceship and
go whooshing through the STARS
And be the first space pilot
who has ever been to MARS!

Your spaceship will get smashed
but you'll be fine with any luck,
And I'll pick up the pieces
in my lovely . . .

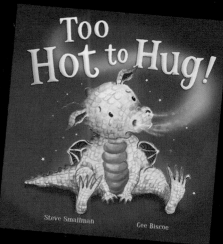
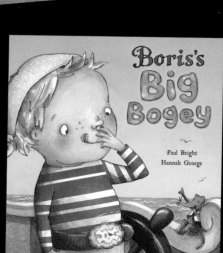